For Samir and Karishma with a million kisses,
and for Rajeev with love
—V.B.

To my son, George, with a kiss
—I.B.

Text copyright © 2004 by Varsha Bajaj
Illustrations copyright © 2004 by Ivan Bates

Little, Brown and Company

Time Warner Book Group
1271 Avenue of the Americas, New York, NY 10020
Visit our Web site at www.lb-kids.com

First Edition

Library of Congress Cataloging-in-Publication Data

Bajaj, Varsha.
    How many kisses do you want tonight? / by Varsha Bajaj ; illustrated by Ivan Bates.—
1st ed.
      p. cm.
    Summary: When bedtime comes, the parents of a girl, a boy, and various animals ask
their children how many kisses they want.
    ISBN 0-316-82381-3
    [1. Kissing—Fiction. 2. Parent and child—Fiction. 3. Bedtime—Fiction. 4.
Animals—Fiction. 5. Counting. 6. Stories in rhyme.] I. Bates, Ivan, ill. II. Title.

PZ8.3.B165Ho 2004
[E]—dc21   2003040269

10 9 8 7 6 5 4 3

SC

Book design by Tracy Shaw

Manufactured in China

The illustrations were done in watercolor and colored pencil on Winsor & Newton Lana paper.
The text was set in Pastonchi, and the display type is Florens.

How Many Kisses Do You Want Tonight?

By Varsha Bajaj

Illustrated by Ivan Bates

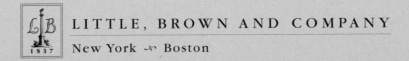

LITTLE, BROWN AND COMPANY
New York ❧ Boston

"How many kisses do you want tonight?"
Daddy Bear growls, cuddling Little Bear tight.

"I want ONE," laughs Little Bear,
"A big, loud kiss on my soft, brown hair."

"How many kisses do you want, young fellow?"
Mommy Duck asks, fluffing Little Duck yellow.

"I want TWO," he says with a quack,

"One on my beak and one on my back."

"How many kisses do you want, my dear?"
Daddy Cat meows in Little Cat's ear.

"I want THREE," purrs Little Cat,
Yawning and curling up on her mat.

"How many kisses do you want, sweetie pie?"
Mommy Butterfly asks her Little Flutterby.

"I want FOUR," Little Butterfly sings,
Folding up his tired, tiny wings.

"How many kisses do you want, pretty mare?"
Daddy Horse asks, nuzzling Little Horse's hair.

"I want FIVE," she says with a neigh,
Settling down in her warm bed of hay.

"How many kisses do you want, Little Pooch?"
Mommy Dog asks with a nudge and a smooch.

"I want SIX," he says with a bark,
Closing his droopy eyes in the dark.

"How many kisses do you want, sweet thing?"
Daddy Bird chirps, stroking Little Bird's wing.

"I want SEVEN," she says with a peep,
Snuggling down in their nest to sleep.

"How many kisses do you want, busy one?"
Mommy Spider asks her Little Spider son.

"I want EIGHT," he says with a giggle,
"One on each leg—I'll try not to wiggle."

"How many kisses do you want, little guy?"
Daddy Snake hisses to Little Snake shy.

"I want NINE," he says with a smile,
Slithering into his grassy pile.

"How many kisses do you want, honey bun?"
Mommy Bunny asks her playful, little one.

"I want TEN," Little Bunny sighs,
"On my floppy ears and my eyes."

"How many kisses do you want, princess
pink?"
Daddy asks his Little Girl with a wink.
"I want a HUNDRED," says Little Girl,
"One on my nose and one on each curl."

"How many kisses do you want, brave knight?"
Mommy asks her Little Boy, hugging him tight.
"I want a MILLION," he says with delight.
Finishing his book, he says good night.

How many kisses do YOU want tonight?